Children Have Got to be Carefully Taught

To Michelle + Mike
never grow up!
Love ya.

To Taylor, my little Hellion.
May you teach your parents well.
All my love, Crazy Aunt Kat.

Children have got to be carefully taught,

of things we all knew but one day forgot.

Children have got to be properly led

to find shapes in clouds
and frogs by the stream,

Of fireflies, stars and wonders in the night,

of wild adventures in far off places:

and stand on their head,

To seek

pots of gold

to frolic in fields

and spray the whipped cream.

and make funny faces,

to play with their food

and pick
at their
braces.

with fantasy, mirth
and little red sleds,

pushed to
extremes,

with everyday people

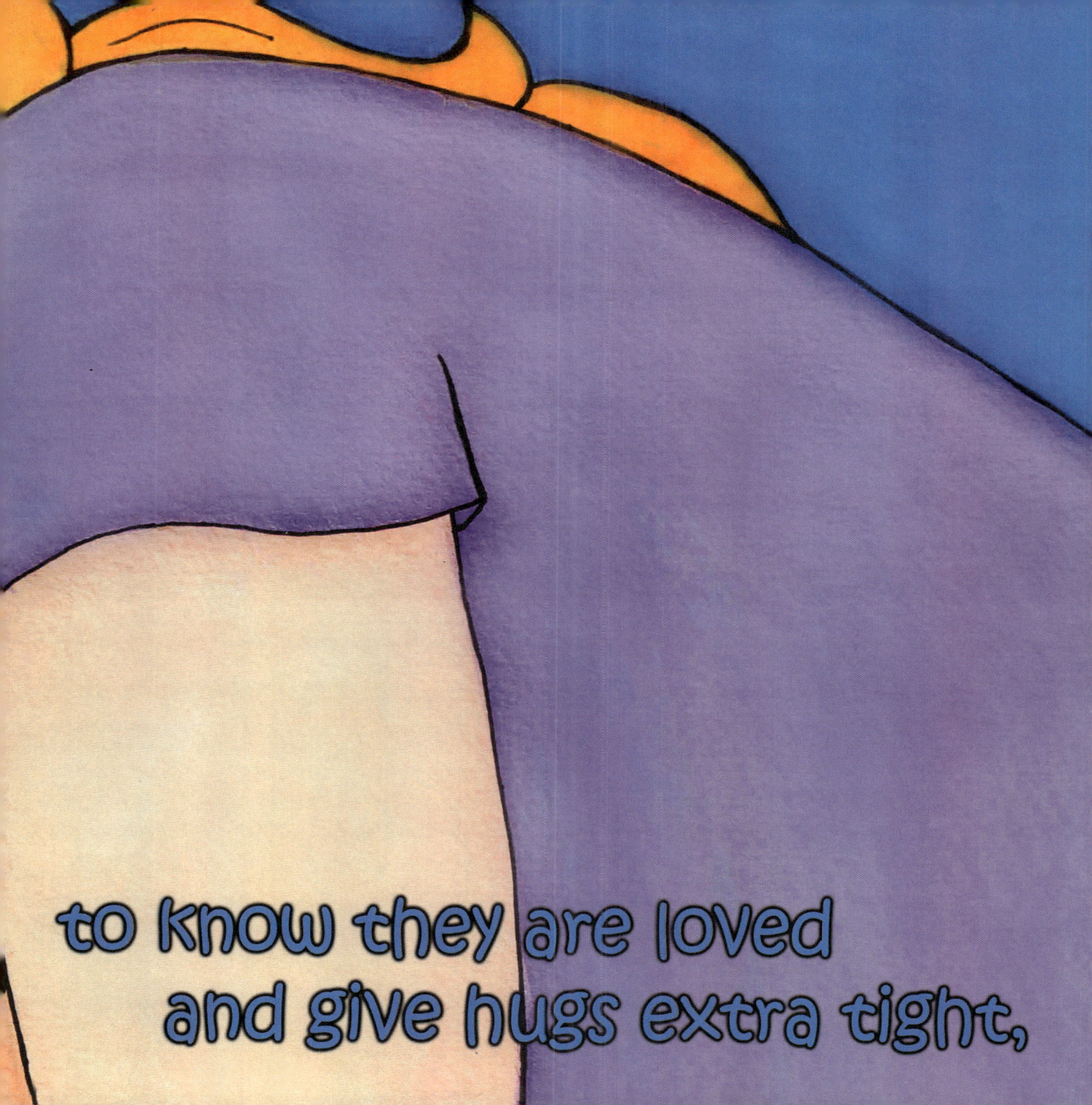

to know they are loved
and give hugs extra tight,

to learn when to let go
and enter life's race,